R🔍CKH🔍UND
SCIENCE
MYSTERIES
10th Anniversary Collection

By Mark H. Newhouse

Illustrations by Denise Gilgannon

Executive Producer . . . . . . Carol Stern
Producer . . . . . . Denise Welborn
Layout Design . . . . . . Stacy Miller
Special Edition . . . . . . Joshua Newhouse

MMX

ISBN-13: 978-1456499426
ISBN-10: 1456499424

marknewhousebooks.com

Rockhound®
Science Mysteries
by Mark H. Newhouse

Book 1

ROCKHOUND FILES: ROCKHOUND'S JUICIEST CASE

Rockhound the detective heard someone tapping at his door. When he opened the door, he was surprised to see ... two wide-eyed pups!

"Hello! I'm Crystal. My brother is Chip. We need a detective."

Rockhound was not used to such young clients.

"What's the problem?" asked Rockhound.

"We're being cheated, but we can't prove it!" Crystal said. "It began when we got that new cafeteria lady, Myrtle. Our other cafeteria ladies were really great, and our lunches were delicious, but now the food Myrtle gives us is terrible."

"Yeah, it's awful! Especially the juice," Chip interrupted. "Yuck!"

"We think she's adding a lot of water to it," explained Crystal. "She charges us for pure juice and keeps the extra money."

"She says we're just puppies and we don't know nothing," Chip yelped.

2

"Anything, Chip. Anything! How many times do I have to correct you?" complained Crystal.

Chip growled, "Anything! Okay?"

Rockhound sighed, "This doesn't sound like a case for a detective. Did you tell your parents?"

"They don't believe us. We have no proof," Crystal replied. "We thought a detective could prove we're right."

"How?" Rockhound asked. "By tasting the juice? I don't see how we can prove that the juice is being monkeyed with. I'm really sorry."

"Let's get going, Chip," Crystal muttered. "He won't help us."

Chip followed along with his sister. "Good-bye, Mr. Detective," he said. "Thank you for listening anyway."

"Dog biscuits!" Rockhound grumbled. "If only there were a way I

4

could help them."

Rockhound decided to visit the Canine School.

At the school, Rockhound followed the scent of kibble until he came to the cafeteria. It looked dark. He thought he was all alone, but suddenly he heard a voice.

He crept inside to take a closer look. He saw a gigantic dog talking on the telephone. She looked like a ghost.

"I think those bratty pups are getting wise to me. I'd better be more careful." Her voice became icy. "I tell you now, nobody better get in my way. Nobody!" Suddenly she whirled toward the door. "I think I heard something!"

She threw the door open and called out, "Is someone there?"

Rockhound jumped under a

table. If that cafeteria creature found him, there would be no telling what might end up in the school lunch the next day!

He held his breath until he heard her speaking on the phone again. Whew! Rockhound's breath rushed out of his lungs.

Rockhound hurried to his car. As he drove away, he tried to think of a way to trap Myrtle.

Suddenly he spotted Crystal. She was licking an ice pop, not missing a drop. Nearby, Chip was slobbering the sticky liquid all over his chin.

"Isn't he a pig?" Crystal teased. "Look at that mess!"

Chip stopped slobbering long enough to make a face at her.

"He's enjoying himself," Rockhound laughed. He explained that he was working on their case, but still couldn't think of a way to prove that the cafeteria juice wasn't pure.

"Taste it," Chip suggested.

"We need scientific proof," explained Rockhound.

"Don't worry," Chip snorted. "You'll figure out something. I've got confidence in you."

Rockhound quietly watched Chip struggling with his ice pop. Suddenly Rockhound gasped. "It's simple! You've given me the answer!"

"Me?" Chip asked, juice trickling down his chin.

"Yes," Rockhound howled, "you and your sticky ice pop have solved the mystery! Why didn't I think of it before?"

"Think of what?" Chip asked.

"A test to prove your juice isn't pure! If I'm right, that cafeteria lady will soon be 'on ice' herself!"

STUDENT PREDICTION PAGE:
What do you think the outcome will be?
Write your prediction on these pages.

_____

_____

_____

_____

_____

_____

_____

_____

_____

9

AND NOW BACK TO OUR STORY...

Rockhound bought a container of pure orange juice and headed back to the school. It was time to confront the conniving cafeteria lady!

"I'd like to perform an experiment for the students," Rockhound explained to Myrtle, the cafeteria lady. "I'm going to make ice pops for the pups."

"How nice," Myrtle wheezed.

Rockhound said, "I'll need some orange juice . . ."

Myrtle grumbled, but got the juice. Rockhound poured it into some paper cups and placed sticks in the cups.

"Oh," Rockhound said, "I forgot one thing. I've brought some of my own orange juice with me." He smiled at her as he poured the juice

into cups and labeled them "100% juice."

Myrtle wondered why he had brought his own juice.

"There," Rockhound announced. "We're ready for the freezer. You know, it amazes me how different liquids freeze at different rates of speed."

Myrtle was suddenly nervous.

"Yessiree," Rockhound chatted, "all this juice should freeze at the same time."

Myrtle was sweating. Her heart was pounding. This dog knew! He was trying to trap her!

Myrtle blurted out, "I have work to do, Mister . . . what did you say your name was?"

"Rockhound," he smiled. "Rockhound the detective."

Myrtle was startled. "Did you say

'detective'?"

Rockhound nodded. Myrtle worked nervously while Rockhound sat calmly waiting. Then Rockhound announced, "It's time to check the cups to see if they're frozen."

Rockhound looked at the cups. "I wonder why that happened! All of your juices are frozen . . . but not the pure orange juice."

Myrtle didn't wait for anything else. She screamed, throwing the tray of juice cups on Rockhound. She ran out of the door with Rockhound holding on.

Suddenly she slammed to a stop and Rockhound fell to the ground. "Let go of me!" she bellowed.

Just then, Myrtle noticed the hallway was clogged with every puppy in the school. She roared, "Get out of my way you brats!"

14

The puppies refused to move. Suddenly Chip, his voice trembling, said, "You're under arrest, cafeteria lady. Rockhound has proven you water down our orange juice. You won't be cheating us anymore."

"I'll bite your ears off," Myrtle growled, showing her teeth.

"I don't think so," Rockhound said, slapping handcuffs on her wrists. "I think your days of bullying these pups are over."

Myrtle collapsed like an emptied bag of flour.

"Well, pups," Rockhound said when it was all over, "I guess this case is closed."

"Yeah," Chip laughed. "You could say it was a tough squeeze."

Crystal playfully swatted Chip across his head while Rockhound laughed.

THE END

15

ROCKHOUND FILES:
THE FIZZLING
FOSSIL PUZZLER

The Weasel Mansion looked dark and unfriendly. It was protected by high, spiked fences and electrified barbed wire.

Rockhound the detective held his identification card up to a security camera by the gate. The gate opened and he walked toward a huge steel door. Suddenly, it opened.

"We must be very careful," W.W. Weasel hissed as he opened the door and led Rockhound down a long hallway to a small, windowless room. A security camera was watching them from a corner of the ceiling.

"I need your help," Weasel whined. "They are trying to steal the DOGOSAURUS!"

So that's it, Rockhound thought. The Dogosaurus! The most valuable fossil in dog history!

"They'll stop at nothing to steal my treasure," Weasel continued.

Rockhound listened as Weasel related the long, involved history of the Dogosaurus Fossil, discovered

accidentally while digging up volcanic rock in Catsylvania.

Rockhound suddenly remembered. The Catsylvanians wanted the fossil back, but Weasel had refused. Now they were in court, fighting over who should own the precious relic.

"The Cats are trying to steal it," Weasel said, staring into Rockhound's face. "You must protect it."

"Why don't you call the police or the FBI? This sounds like a job for them," explained Rockhound.

"By the time they help, it will be too late," Weasel answered. "You are my only hope."

"I don't know," Rockhound answered. Something about this case was fishy.

Weasel smiled, "Even if you could help just until other arrangements are made."

Rockhound didn't like Weasel's smile. "Why in the world would the Catsylvanians steal what they'll probably win in court?" he asked.

Weasel snarled, "They won't win! The Dogosaurus is mine! Mine!" Rockhound jumped out of his seat.

Weasel calmed down. "Will you help me?"

"Show me the fossil," Rockhound said, not sure that he wanted to get involved.

"Impossible," Weasel declared. "Security reasons. You understand."

"I'm sorry," Rockhound said, moving toward the door, "I can't guard what I can't see."

"Wait. Please wait." Weasel circled behind Rockhound. "Be reasonable."

Rockhound was losing patience. "Call the FBI," he grunted.

"No!" Weasel shouted. "I want you! With you, I know the fossil will be safe."

Rockhound liked compliments, but not this time. "Do I see the fossil or not?" he demanded.

Weasel grumbled, "Very well. I will fetch it."

Rockhound didn't trust this character . . . something was definitely wrong. Suddenly he thought of a plan. "Where can I get some tea?" he asked, trying to sound friendlier.

Weasel looked surprised. "How thoughtless of me," he murmured. "What would you like?"

Rockhound smiled and requested, "Tea and fresh lemon please."

His host nodded and left the room.

Rockhound got ready.

Soon, Weasel returned with a

22

silver tray carrying tea and several slices of lemon. "I'll be back in a minute," Weasel muttered as he left the room to fetch the rare fossil.

Alone again, Rockhound turned his back to the video camera. He quickly placed a lemon slice into his coat pocket. He now had a way to test his suspicions. He sipped a little of the tea and made a face. Tea always tasted bitter to him.

"Here it is," Weasel announced, hugging a small wood box. "The famous Dogosaurus Fossil."

Weasel shoved the tea tray out the door, his eyes never leaving the locked box. He unlocked the box and gently placed the fossil on a clean cloth on the table.

Rockhound tried to hide his amazement. It was hard to believe that an object barely six inches long

could be of such value.

"To the uneducated, such as yourself," Weasel announced, "it looks worthless . . . like a common stone found in any backyard, not the remains of some prehistoric canine trapped in a volcanic flow. It's priceless!"

Rockhound moved to touch the fossil.

"No," Weasel growled. "Don't touch!"

"Give me a break," Rockhound barked. "I've got to examine this thing before I agree to protect it."

"Do be careful," Weasel reluctantly agreed. "It is priceless."

"Don't worry," Rockhound said. "I'll be gentle."

Rockhound reached to touch the stone. "Oh," he said suddenly.

"Something wrong?" Weasel was

alarmed.

Rockhound smiled, "It's nothing. My hands are sticky . . . from the tea. Have you a towel?"

Weasel looked annoyed. "I'll get something," he grumbled. "Wait here!"

Weasel scurried out muttering.

Rockhound quickly grabbed the lemon from his pocket and squeezed several drops over the fossil. . . . He stared down at the stone. Slowly, he smiled. His suspicions had been correct.

27

STUDENT PREDICTION PAGE:
What do you think the outcome will be?
Write your prediction on these pages.

_____

_____

_____

_____

_____

_____

_____

_____

_____

28

29

AND NOW BACK TO OUR STORY...

In the dimly lit room, Rockhound had to bend down close to the fossil to be sure. The lemon juice was bubbling on the surface of the fossil. His hunch had been correct. He quickly tried it again. It was definitely fizzing. He quickly rubbed the lemon juice with his finger until the juice was invisible. Suddenly, the door opened with explosive speed. "Here," Weasel gasped, holding a paper towel.

Rockhound wiped his paws. He then bent closer, pretending to examine the fossil.

"Thank you," he said after several minutes, "I've seen enough."

Weasel watched Rockhound's every move. "You are satisfied?" he asked, locking away the Dogosaurus.

Rockhound smiled. "Oh, yes, I'm

31

completely satisfied."

"Good," Weasel said, rushing Rock-hound outside. "You will begin now?"

"I need to get some help," Rockhound said, "then we'll be set."

"Good," Weasel said, a sly look on his face. "I feel much better."

"So do I," Rockhound replied, walking toward his car to phone the police.

The police arrested Weasel for stealing and selling the real Dogosaurus.

"But how did you know?" Weasel yelped.

"Detective secret," Rockhound said as they took Weasel away.

"How did you know?" his friend Captain Chihuahua asked. "This fossil looks real to me."

Rockhound explained he had been suspicious from the first. He couldn't understand why Weasel needed a detective. The FBI or Police would have done the job, and for free. "I figured he was pulling a fast one."

"What was his plan?" Captain Chihuahua asked.

"Well, the only thing that made sense," Rockhound continued, "was that Weasel had stolen the real Dogosaurus and sold it.

"I guessed that he wanted to convince the Catsylvanians that the fossil they would win in court was the true Dogosaurus. Weasel figured they wouldn't question it if he actually paid to have it protected. He just didn't count on me figuring out it was phony!"

"That was a good guess," Captain Chihuahua said, "but how did you know you were right?"

"I was lucky," Rockhound admitted. "I couldn't have been sure if I hadn't remembered that the genuine fossil was made of VOLCANIC rock. There was LIMESTONE in the fake."

"But how did you know that?" Chihuahua was puzzled.

"It was the bubbles," Rockhound explained. "I remembered from my elementary school science classes that when you drop lemon juice on limestone, it bubbles. Volcanic rock wouldn't have fizzed like that. Try it yourself with lemon juice or vinegar. If it hadn't had limestone in it, I would have had to try some other tests."

The Captain laughed, "You mean it really was 'elementary' this time?"

"I guess it was," Rockhound laughed. "You might say Wily Weasel's fossil fizzled!"

 THE 🦴 END

35

ROCKHOUND FILES: JACK AND THE GREENSTALKS

Rockhound the detective stared at his host. The small reddish squirrel was seated on a chair in the center of a room whose floor was completely covered by a thin layer of white flour.

"I don't understand how they're doing it," his host muttered through clenched teeth. "I have taken every precaution I can think of . . . and they're still dying. It must be ghosts."

Rockhound had seen for himself the incredible alarm systems and the electronic gates that protected the house. Only a ghost could break into this house, he thought.

"Night and day, I stand guard. Every day I check the floor for footprints. Nothing! Absolutely nothing! And yet they're dying! Someone is killing them." The squirrel looked nervously around the room.

Rockhound found himself glancing nervously around the room as well. "Jack," he said in a calm voice, "who is dying?"

Jack looked up with large redlined eyes. "My precious babies. My wife left me to protect them while she takes care of her sick mother." He looked like he was about to cry. "I've tried everything, and I've failed."

"Babies!" Rockhound gasped. This was serious. "Where are these babies now?" Rockhound asked his host.

Jack stood up slowly. "Come with me," he said. "I'll show you." He led Rockhound toward the far wall of the room and shut off yet another alarm. He slid away a wall panel to reveal the huge steel door of a vault.

Rockhound gasped, "You keep your babies in a safe?"

"I just wanted to protect my wife's babies."

Rockhound glared at his host. "Whoever heard of keeping babies in a safe?" he growled as Jack turned the combination and pulled the handle. Jack guided him inside. "It's dark in here," Rockhound muttered.

Jack flicked on the lights.

"So where are these babies of yours?" Rockhound asked, angry that anyone would keep babies in a dark and airless safe.

"Here they are . . . my precious ones," Jack said as he pointed to a shelf at the back of the safe.

"They're . . . plants!" Rockhound shouted. "Your 'babies' are plants?"

The squirrel nodded his head. "They are my wife's most precious possessions. They're extremely rare and very expensive. She'll kill me when she sees them."

Rockhound examined the plants. They were indeed dying.

"How could anyone get near them?" the squirrel kept asking. "Do

you think it's poison?"

Rockhound was thinking. It didn't seem possible that anyone could bypass all of Jack Squirrel's alarms and poison his "babies," and yet, the plants were definitely dying. He stepped back out of the vault and stared at the flour-covered floor. "No footprints ever?" he asked Jack who was resealing the dark safe.

"None," Jack whined. "I tell you it's ghosts!"

"Ghosts," Rockhound said softly. "I don't think so."

"Then who?" Jack Squirrel asked. "Who is killing my plants?"

STUDENT PREDICTION PAGE:
What do you think the outcome will be?
Write your prediction on these pages.

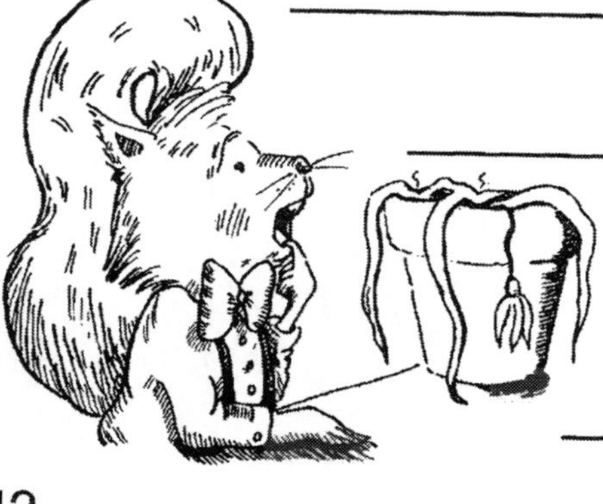

_____

_____

_____

_____

_____

_____

_____

_____

_____

AND NOW BACK TO OUR STORY...

Rockhound looked at the squirrel with sympathetic eyes. "I think someone is killing your plants . . . I think it's you."

"Are you crazy?" the squirrel began to scream. "Me! I'd never do anything to hurt my babies!"

Rockhound sighed, "But you did. In trying to protect your plants, you almost killed them."

"How?" the upset squirrel cried out. "I wouldn't harm a hair on their little green leaves!"

Rockhound smiled, "Plants need sunlight and air to grow. You locked them in a dark and airless vault. Without air and light, your plants began to die."

The squirrel's mouth dropped open. "Air and light . . . You mean I was killing my own plants?"

45

Rockhound smiled, "You didn't mean to. Take them out of the safe and I think they'll be just fine."

Jack Squirrel grabbed Rockhound's paw. "Thank you! Thank you! How can I ever repay you?"

Rockhound smiled and said, "Just name one of the babies after me."

In a year's time, a beautiful Rock garden was thriving at Jack's house. It was filled with a variety of plants like Dog's-tooth Violets, Paw-paws, Horehound and Dog Fennel and was shaded by graceful Dogwood trees.

THE END

Rockhound™
Science Mysteries
by Mark H. Newhouse

Book 2

ROCKHOUND FILES: THE CASE OF THE ROTTEN EGG

"Is something wrong?" Rockhound asked, as he joined his old friend Captain Chihuahua at the entrance of the Dog House Hotel.

Chihuahua was shaking. "It's just terrible. Terrible! I don't know how it could have happened."

"What happened?" Rockhound asked as Chihuahua led him to the elevator.

"It appears he fell . . . he fell right off the wall," Chihuahua moaned as the elevator reached the twenty-first floor of the hotel.

"Who fell?" Rockhound asked as Chihuahua walked by Officer Peke guarding a door.

"Anyone try to leave?" Chihuahua asked Peke.

"No one, Captain," Peke replied. "Everyone's in the room just like you wanted."

"Everyone but H.D.," Chihuahua moaned.

"Who is H.D.?" Rockhound asked as he noticed three strangers seated silently in the large room.

Chihuahua looked surprised. "You have never heard of H.D.?" he asked.

Rockhound tried to think.

Chihuahua grunted, "Humpty Dumpty. You HAVE heard of him, haven't you?"

Rockhound let a whistle escape through his razor-sharp teeth. "Humpty Dumpty," he growled. "Is that who you're so upset about? Wasn't he the leader of the Rotten Egg Gang?"

Chihuahua grunted once again. "Hey, I never liked him either, but I suspect that someone in this room pushed him off that wall. Now he's lying on the ground all cracked up!"

"Are you telling me that you think someone here pushed him off that wall?" Rockhound asked as he stared at the strangers in the room.

"Yep," Chihuahua said. "Humpty Dumpty sat on a wall. Humpty Dumpty had a great fall."

"Oh, boy," Rockhound said as he glanced over the terrace wall. "If he fell from here, he must have been really scrambled!"

Chihuahua exclaimed, "All the king's horses and all the king's men couldn't put him together again!"

"But I still don't understand it,"

4

Rockhound frankly blurted out. "Why should you care about the leader of the Rotten Egg Gang?"

Chihuahua leaned in close to Rockhound and whispered in his ear, "He was going to tell us everything he knew about Weasel and his rival gang of crooks."

"Weasel?" Rockhound snarled. "So you think Weasel had something to do with this?"

"I sure do," Chihuahua growled. "I think Weasel hired one of these suspects as an assassin. I think Weasel knew that H.D. was ready to tell us everything he knew about Weasel's gang. Weasel had already cooked Eggs Benedict and Cheese Omelet, two members of H.D.'s Rotten Egg Gang. H.D. was scared and warned us that he was going to be fried next. That's why we had him locked in this hotel room."

"Okay," Rockhound said thoughtfully, "but just who are these three characters?"

Chihuahua smiled. "We got here

soon enough after the crime to make sure that nobody had a chance to leave. One of the individuals in this room pushed H.D. off the wall."

"Good work," Rockhound smiled. "You've got your killer."

"Sort of," Chihuahua said as he bit his lip. "I'm afraid we have one slight problem."

Rockhound looked at his friend. "Let me guess. You still don't know which of these characters did it."

Chihuahua grunted. "They've all got good reasons for being here. I was hoping you could listen to their stories and help me figure out who did it."

Rockhound looked at the faces in the room. Sometimes he wished that crooks actually looked like crooks. "Okay," he finally said, "let's get started."

Chihuahua led him into the hotel suite and sat him down at a table. One by one Chihuahua brought the witnesses into the room to meet with Rockhound.

The first witness was the cook. "I was busy making breakfast," the cook said. "I knew nothing until I heard someone scream in the other room."

"What were you cooking?" the detective asked. His keen nose had picked up the scent of bacon on the cook's apron.

"Bacon," the cook said, eyeing the detective. Rockhound sent her to the living room and then watched as the nurse sat down before him. She explained that she had been worried about H.D.'s health and had given him an examination earlier that morning.

"And did you find anything?" Rockhound asked, writing in his notepad.

"His heartbeat was very fast," she said. "He complained he was feeling dizzy. I'm really not surprised that he fell. He never kept to his diets. Humpty Dumpty was an accident waiting to happen."

Rockhound thanked her and

watched as the final witness, H.D.'s bodyguard, moved into the room. He was a huge saint bernard, with large muscles and a mean face. "I got no time to talk to you," he snarled. "I don't know nothing about this." He started to leave.

"Sit down!" Rockhound ordered, not liking this huge dog one bit. "I have some questions for you, and you are going to take the time to answer them or find yourself in the pound."

The bodyguard growled. For just a second, Rockhound thought the big dog was going to smash him with his gigantic paw. Then the body-guard sat down, making the chair sag with his weight.

"Did anyone other than the cook, nurse, and yourself meet with H.D. this morning?" Rockhound asked.

As the saint bernard thought, his heavy brow wrinkled as if he was in pain. "Naw," he finally said. "I'm sure we were the only ones to see him. Nobody else."

"The cook went into her room afterwards?" Rockhound asked, his keen eyes studying the face of the large dog. He wondered if the bodyguard realized how close he was to being arrested.

"Yeah," the bodyguard mumbled, "I think so. H.D. wasn't feeling so good. That's why he had the nurse. The cook came into the room like she always did to give H.D. his breakfast in bed. When the cook left, the nurse usually came in."

"Did you go in with them?" Rockhound asked.

"I used to," the big dog answered, "but they always went in before and nothing ever happened. I figured it was okay, so I didn't follow them in today. Did I do the wrong thing?" the big dog asked.

Rockhound sighed. This big dog just didn't seem like he would have hurt his boss. "Okay," he said more kindly, "tell me what you can about the cook and the nurse."

The big dog scratched his head. "I don't know what to tell you. Every day the cook would bring H.D. breakfast and then the nurse would give him an examination. I watched so many times that I swear I could do the exam myself." The dog let out a huge laugh. "Want to see how I can take your pulse?" The dog didn't wait for an answer, but grabbed Rockhound's paw and slammed his thumb down on Rockhound's wrist. He "listened" for his pulse.

"You need a watch to take my pulse," Rockhound said feeling the thumb grind into his skin. "Ouch! You're hurting me," Rockhound said as he pulled his wrist free.

"I'm sorry," the saint bernard mumbled. "I did it like the nurse, but I guess I need more practice."

Rockhound rubbed his wrist and sighed. Three suspects and not one clue. Maybe H.D. had just fallen off the wall after all. Rockhound stared down at his wrist. "Wait a minute!" he called to Chihuahua. "I think I've got the killer."

"I didn't do it!" the saint bernard said, jumping to his paws. "I didn't do it!"

"I know!" Rockhound shouted as he raced into the other room. "I know you didn't do it."

"Then who did commit this crime? Who could have killed Humpty Dumpty?" Chihuahua asked as he and Rockhound approached the cook and the nurse . . .

STUDENT PREDICTION PAGE
What do *you* think the outcome will be?
Write your prediction on these pages.

_____

_____

_____

_____

_____

_____

_____

_____

_____

_____

AND NOW BACK TO OUR STORY...

Rockhound had asked Captain Chihuahua to hold out his paw.

Chihuahua looked confused.

"Now," he said as he signaled the bodyguard, "I want you to take the Captain's pulse exactly the same way that you took my pulse."

The saint bernard looked worried. "But I already told you I didn't do it."

Rockhound smiled patiently. "Please just do what I asked."

The bodyguard stood up and took the Captain's tiny paw. He pressed his thumb on the Captain's bony wrist.

"Good," Rockhound said. "How did you learn how to do that?"

The bodyguard looked proud of himself. "I watched 'Nursey' there," the bodyguard replied.

Rockhound held his wrist before the nurse. "Would you please take my pulse?"

She took Rockhound's paw and pressed her thumb on his wrist.

"Thank you," Rockhound said.

"Captain Chihuahua, if you check this character's nursing papers, I think you'll find they're fake. This impostor is Weasel's hired assassin, meant to keep Humpty Dumpty from spilling the beans about Weasel's gang."

The nurse sputtered, broke free of Rockhound, and ran straight into Officer Peke. "How did you know?" she blubbered as Officer Peke led her away.

"How DID you know?" Chihuahua asked.

Rockhound smiled. "We knew one of the three in the room was the killer, but it wasn't until I saw the nurse use her thumb to take my pulse that I knew for sure she was a phony. No real nurse would use the thumb because it has a pulse of its own, which makes it hard to feel the real pulsebeat. The bodyguard tipped me off when he tried to take my pulse incorrectly. He said he learned how by watching the nurse."

"You mean," the saint bernard said, "I helped you solve this case?"

Rockhound laughed, "I guess you did. You could say that you really 'fingered' the killer."

Chihuahua just groaned and rubbed his sore wrist.

THE END

16

ROCKHOUND FILES: THE MULTIMILLION DOLLAR MOUSEY MYSTERY

Rockhound laughed out loud when he looked at Captain Chihuahua, dressed in a wildly-colored striped shirt, baggy shorts, knee socks and a camera hanging from his neck. "Don't you think you overdid your disguise a bit?" Rockhound teased.

Chihuahua let out a low growl, "Will you stop bothering me about my outfit, and pay attention? The director of this museum will have our badges if something happens to that mouse!"

Rockhound sighed and tried to concentrate on the tour guide. "And here," she announced, "we have 'Three Blind Mice Climbing a Ladder,' a very fine example of modern art."

"Looks like a lot of cheese to me," Chihuahua grumbled. "I just can't believe how valuable some of this stuff is."

"And now ladies and gentlemen," the tour guide announced, "you are in for a real treat."

"This is it," Chihuahua whispered as he pinched Rockhound.

"Stop pinching me," Rockhound snarled. "I hate when you do that!"

"You are about to see the most valuable work of art in the entire animal world!" the guide said as she led the group into the room. "It is here on a brief loan from the Mouse Museum in Italy. You are fortunate to have this opportunity to see this famous work of art."

"Okay! Enough talk," Chihuahua growled.

The tour guide continued, "I am very pleased to present to you the 'Mona Mousey,' drawn by Leonardo da Mousey nearly 500 years ago."

Rockhound stared at the drawing he and Chihuahua were hired to guard during its loan to the Cultured Cheese Museum. Although it was not very large, it had been a target of thieves throughout its history. He always wondered what was so special about this 500 year-old drawing of an unknown female mouse. Now, as he stood face to face with the "Mona Mousey," he was almost hypnotized by her eyes . . . they seemed to be looking slightly toward the left . . . yet at the same time seemed to follow him as he viewed the drawing from different points in the room.

THE "MONA MOUSEY" BY LEONARDO DA MOUSEY

"Some people say," the tour guide continued, "that it is the smile of the 'Mona Mousey' that drives people to own her no matter what the risk. Others say the eyes seem to be aimed to the right, and yet have the ability to follow you anywhere in the room."

Rockhound was only half listening . . . he was totally fascinated by the small square drawing.

"It's hard to believe," Chihuahua whispered, "that a drawing the size of a piece of loose-leaf paper can be worth millions."

Rockhound was deep in thought. Suddenly he turned to Chihuahua. "Did the tour guide say that the eyes were turned to the right or. . . did she say left?"

Chihuahua shrugged. "I've no idea," he said. "What difference does it make?"

Rockhound turned back to the drawing. There's no doubt about it, he thought, her eyes are aimed to the left.

Rockhound signaled Chihuahua and they left the room.

"Something wrong?" Chihuahua asked, as he followed Rockhound to the museum library.

"I'm not sure," Rockhound said. "It could be nothing. The tour guide might have made a mistake . . . I'm just going to look in a couple of art books to check something out." Rockhound began to search the index of the books for a picture of the famous drawing.

Rockhound sighed, "I think we've got trouble. I think the drawing in

MOUSEY &
MOUSEY

the museum is a fake."

Chihuahua blustered, "But...it can't be! We're here to protect it!"

Rockhound studied the drawing again. "There's no doubt about it," he whispered. "The museum's drawing is a fake."

"But it looks perfect to me," Chihuahua argued. "And besides, nobody can get near it long enough to make a decent fake."

"I don't know how it was done," Rockhound whispered, "but this drawing is definitely a fake."

Chihuahua groaned. "What do we do now?"

Rockhound had to think. "I don't think we should tell anyone yet. Maybe the thief is still here."

Rockhound began to look for clues. As he ran his paw over the top of the glass display case under the drawing, he suddenly felt something sticky. He looked through his magnifying glass and saw the trace of some kind of sticky substance. It made a nearly invisible line, about a foot long on the glass counter.

He stared at the drawing again. "I can't believe you're not for real," he said to the silent mouse.

"It's time to see the museum director," Chihuahua said rather nervously. "We've got to let her know."

Rockhound and Chihuahua waited in the office of Director Rodentus. It was a large, neat room. The dark paneled walls were covered with many photographs protected by glass frames.

Rockhound got up and walked around the room, studying all the photos. He was impressed by the many photos of famous people. The director was certainly popular. "She's amazing," he said to Chihuahua who was worried about how he was going to tell this 'amazing' lady that she was missing an amazing work of art. "Look at all these photographs of her posing with celebrities," Rockhound said. "There's even one with Lassie!"

Chihuahua reluctantly got up from his chair and walked over to the wall. "You're right," he said. "Director Rodentus sure enjoys being in the spotlight."

Rockhound nodded.

"What do you think was over here?" Chihuahua asked, looking at a nail sticking out of a square-shaped blank spot on the wall.

"Who knows," Rockhound said returning to the desk.

"The wall is faded here . . . something had to have been here," Chihuahua laughed suddenly. "Hey, listen to me! I'm starting to sound like you!"

Rockhound laughed. Suddenly he gasped. "Let me see that," he said rushing to the wall. He took out his tape measure. "The size of loose-leaf paper . . . maybe a bit larger . . ."

Rockhound quickly raced back to the director's desk. He hurriedly searched the top and then searched through the drawers.

"Are you crazy?" Chihuahua hissed. "What are you doing?"

Suddenly Rockhound smiled. In his paws was a package of clay and what looked like a thin sheet of glass . . . about the size of loose-leaf paper. "Captain," Rockhound said, "I think you've solved the case."

Chihuahua was still shocked by Rockhound's search through the director's desk. He stared at the door expecting it to burst open at any second, revealing a snarling Rodentus.

Rockhound swept the top of the director's desk clean of clutter and pulled out a sheet of plain, white paper from a drawer. "Let's create some art!" he announced.

"What are you doing?" Chihuahua asked. "That paper is the property of Director Rodentus!"

"Watch this," Rockhound said as he found a drawing in a magazine and placed it on the desk, next to the sheet of white paper.

"I don't see anything," the Captain said.

"You will," Rockhound said. "You will!"

STUDENT PREDICTION PAGE
What do *you* think the outcome will be?
Write your prediction on these pages.

_____

_____

_____

_____

_____

_____

_____

_____

_____

AND NOW BACK TO OUR STORY...

Rockhound molded the clay, forming a line on the desk between the two pieces of paper. He then took the rectangular glass and pressed it's edge into the clay until it was able to stand by itself.

Chihuahua sighed. "I still don't get it."

Rockhound turned to Chihuahua. "Can you draw?"

Chihuahua laughed, "I'm terrible. I can't even draw a crooked line."

"Come here," Rockhound said. "I'm going to turn you into an artist. Look through the glass from this side." He showed Chihuahua how to look through the glass from the side of the original drawing. "What do you see?"

Chihuahua gasped, "It's the drawing . . . I can see the drawing on the blank sheet of paper."

"Good," Rockhound said. "Now just trace what you see."

"That's amazing," Chihuahua said

after he saw his finished sketch.

"That's how the fake drawing of the 'Mona Mousey' was done so quickly," Rockhound announced. "The sticky line on the table was the clay used to make the glass stand and the glass . . . well, you discovered the missing photograph on the wall. The director removed it from the wall so she could use the glass to make the fake drawing."

Director Rodentus could hardly believe she had been caught. "I had to do it," she cried. "I wanted to be accepted by my celebrity friends. With all the money I was going to get for that drawing, they could never turn me down from the Big Cheese Society. It's really hard for a rat to make friends. I had to . . . I had to!"

"But how did you know it was a fake?" Chihuahua asked after Director Rodentus was led away.

"Look in the glass again," Rockhound said. "Do you notice anything about the original drawing and your drawing that is different?"

Chihuahua looked carefully. "They look exactly alike . . . hey, wait a minute . . . I do see something . . . my drawing is facing the wrong way." Chihuahua smiled, "That's why you asked me about the eyes."

"The director must have been in such a hurry that she didn't notice that the eyes on her forgery were looking the wrong way," Rockhound

laughed.

"And she hired us to make it look like the real drawing was still here." Chihuahua shook his head. "I guess being surrounded by all those famous and rich people was just too much for her."

"Now that we know Director Rodentus took the real 'Mona Mousey,' we'll recover it and put it back in it s place in the museum. I guess we're out of the art business," Rockhound said.

"Oh I don't know," Chihuahua grinned. "I think I could become quite an artist with this trick you taught me."

"Oh no," Rockhound muttered as he imagined what Chihuahua would look like if he tried dressing like an artist.

THE END

ROCKHOUND FILES: THE STRANGE CASE OF DR. JERKYL AND DR. HIDE

Rockhound shivered. The house looked as if it had eyes; cold, yellow eyes staring down at the fenced-in yard below.

"I was hoping it was you," a tall, wiry wolfhound proclaimed with a Russian accent, brushing a bony paw through his thick fur. "I'm Dr. Hide and we must hurry."

"I've heard of you," Rockhound said, noting that Hide's hair looked rather knotted and wild. "You're the inventor of . . . of . . ."

"Monster Juice," Hide gushed, "the world's number-one-selling soft drink."

Rockhound recited the famous slogan, "'To drink anything else is simply monstrous.'"

"Oh, I do hate that slogan," Hide muttered, running a paw through his wildly flowing hair again. "But this is not why I've sent for you, Rockhound." Hide cast his strange, wild eyes all about the hall and then held his paw up to his lips. "We must speak very quietly or he might hear us."

"Who?" Rockhound asked, watching as Hide gripped the door and then threw it open, checking to see if anyone was listening.

"Why, Dr. Jerkyl, of course," Hide said gnashing his teeth together. "He spies on everything I do."

"Who is Dr. Jerkyl?" Rockhound asked, finding himself now running a paw through his own fur. *It's catching,* he thought as he forced his paw back to his pocket.

Hide whirled around, his white lab coat swirling. "Jerkyl is sneaky and calculating," he declared, his eyes opened wide. "He is stealing my precious new and improved Monster Juice . . . the drink that will destroy my competition." When he leaned toward Rockhound, the detective noticed Hide's breath smelled of Monster Juice and his lips were bright blue. "They're paying him to stop me from producing my new Monster Juice! I know that Jerkyl is stealing my newest creation, and he's doing it right under my nose!"

"Well, why don't you fire him?" Rockhound asked.

Hide looked badly shaken. "I can't. After working for me for years he knows all my secrets. Besides, I have no proof he is stealing! I must have proof!"

Rockhound thought the whole thing sounded crazy. "Why would anyone want to steal some soda pop?" Rockhound asked, wishing he had anything else to drink but Monster Juice in his paw right now.

Hide's voice became shrill. "Soda pop! Soda is big business and my new Monster Juice is top secret!"

Rockhound wished he could stop Hide from screaming at him. "Okay," he said, "how do you think this Dr. Jerkyl is stealing your new improved Monster Juice?"

Hide suddenly turned icy cold. "If I knew that, Mr. Detective, I wouldn't need you!"

Rockhound nearly fell off his chair. This guy was crazy. "Can you please show me where you keep this Monster Junk . . . I mean, Monster JUICE," he corrected quickly.

Hide hissed at him like an angry snake. He led him down a long hall. "My lab," Hide announced, pointing his bony paw at a door just inches away.

Rockhound heard a noise inside. "There's someone there," he grunted.

Suddenly the door opened and a huge German shepherd in an enormous lab coat filled the doorway.

Hide turned pale as the gigantic Jerkyl stared down at him. "What are you doing here?" Hide finally demanded, trying to see behind the large dog's body into the lab.

"Just tidying up a bit," Jerkyl answered in a reedy voice. "Can't stand a messy lab, you know." Jerkyl's huge body was still blocking the door.

Hide pushed past Jerkyl. "Where is it?" demanded Hide, holding up an empty test tube tray. "What have you done with my new Monster Juice 2?"

Jerkyl shrugged, removed his lab coat and put on a sport jacket. Turning to Rockhound he said, "He's mad, you know. Quite mad. He has this crazy idea that I'm stealing from him . . . as if anybody could steal anything from this lab without old snoopy-drawers noticing." Jerkyl laughed and walked away, looking very dressed-up with a large blue carnation in his jacket's lapel.

Hide was rushing about the lab, checking every drawer, every shelf, everywhere. Rockhound was beginning to wonder if maybe Jerkyl was right about him. Suddenly Hide began to moan and shake. "Oh no.

It's gone. It's gone. It's all gone!" Hide turned toward Rockhound, a mad-dog expression on his face. "Go after him! He must have it with him! There's no other way!"

"Impossible," Rockhound said firmly. "I saw him. There was no way he could have stolen your precious Monster Juice. I just saw him leave empty handed."

Hide held his paws pitifully before Rockhound's eyes. "Then how do you explain these empty test tubes that were once filled with Monster Juice!" he asked.

"But I tell you I saw him," Rockhound protested. "There's no way that he could have stolen that secret soda. He wasn't carrying anything! May I look inside the lab again?" Rockhound asked, not sure any longer what to believe.

Hide nodded. "But there's nothing there," he said in a raspy voice. He looked exhausted.

Rockhound entered the lab. He saw barred windows on the other side. He placed his paws on the bars and pulled. They were solid. "Could you please move all these plants?" he asked as he tried to get a better grip. "I've never seen so many plants in one place. They're everywhere!" Suddenly, Rockhound aimed his eyes around the lab. "Plants!" he exclaimed loudly. "Plants!"

Hide jumped backwards.

Rockhound wondered, could Jerkyl be this clever? "Wasn't Jerkyl wearing a carnation?" he shouted at Hide. "It was blue, wasn't it?"

"Why yes, I think so," the startled Hide replied. "He's become quite fond of plants and flowers lately."

"Lately," Rockhound muttered. "Plants! Carnations!" Rockhound whirled around. "Why, Dr. Hide!" he exclaimed. "Look around you!"

Hide turned nervously around the room. He shrugged his shoulders.

"Hide," Rockhound said, excitement growing, "your Monster Juice is right here!"

STUDENT PREDICTION PAGE
What do *you* think the outcome will be?
Write your prediction on these pages.

_____

_____

_____

_____

_____

_____

_____

_____

_____

_____

"You're crazy!" Hide backed away from the detective. "There's nothing here! I tell you he's already taken it all!"

Rockhound pushed Hide toward the window ledge. "Look all around you. Look at these carnations."

"So what?" Hide screamed, trying to break free.

Rockhound smiled and spoke slowly. "These plants are helping to steal your Monster Juice."

Rockhound took a piece of celery out of a glass. "Let's take a closer look at Jerkyl's plants and maybe you'll understand." He cut open the stem. "Look very closely. See those stripes..."

Hide stared at the blue stripes on the celery stalk. "They're blue," Hide said thoughtfully. "Just like the carnation Jerkyl was wearing . . . just like my MONSTER JUICE!"

"There's your missing Monster Juice," Rockhound said triumphantly.

"You did say that Dr. Jerkyl was sneaky, didn't you? Well, I have to agree. Anyone who could get plants to do his dirty work is definitely the sneakiest of sneaks."

"He may be sneaky, but no match for Rockhound," Hide laughed when Jerkyl was arrested a few minutes later by Captain Chihuahua.

"But how did he do it?" Captain Chihuahua asked as he sipped at his glass of Monster Juice.

"It was so incredibly clever," Rockhound explained. "Instead of water, Jerkyl gave the plants the Monster Juice 2. He knew that the plants would soak it up. He planned to take the samples to the Doggy Drink Company where they would analyze the formula in their labs. Then they'd make their own new drink before Dr. Hide could get his out on the market." Rockhound then held up a blue-striped stalk for the captain to see.

"The only stripes Dr. Jerkyl will see now are the stripes on his prison uniform," Rockhound joked to his friend. "I guess I really earned my 'celery' this time."

Captain Chihuahua groaned. He wished Dr. Hide would now invent a secret formula to cure Rockhound of his 'bad jokeitis.'

THE END

Rockhound®
Science Mysteries
by Mark H. Newhouse

Book 3

ROCKHOUND FILES: THE FRAZZLED FORTUNE TELLER

"Do you believe in the supernatural?" Captain Chihuahua asked Rockhound.

"Not really," Rockhound answered. Rockhound never suspected Chihuahua was superstitious.

"That's kind of a strange thing to ask."

Chihuahua fidgeted in his seat. "I need a favor," he said so softly that Rockhound almost didn't hear him. "But I don't want you to laugh when I tell you what it is." Chihuahua looked nervous.

"I won't," Rockhound said, wondering what his friend could possibly need. "I won't laugh."

Chihuahua sighed, "I want you to visit a fortune teller with me."

"A . . . what!" Rockhound exclaimed.

"A fortune teller," Chihuahua repeated. "I want you to accompany me to a séance. You know, it's an event when someone tries to contact the spirits for advice."

"You must be joking," Rockhound said, struggling hard not to laugh.

"That's not all," Chihuahua mumbled.

"What do you mean?" Rockhound asked suspiciously, his ears straining to pick up every word.

Chihuahua hesitated, "We have to be incognito. You'll have to wear a dress and a wig."

"What?" Rockhound exploded.

"We're going to pretend you're my wife," Chihuahua blurted.

Rockhound couldn't help it. He burst into laughter. When he saw Chihuahua wasn't laughing, he stopped. "You are kidding. This is a big joke. Right?"

"I wish," Chihuahua responded weakly. "It's the only way I could think of sneaking you in."

"No way," Rockhound snarled. "Just forget it!"

Chihuahua watched patiently as Rockhound carried on, ranting and raving that he would never wear such a silly costume. Finally Chihuahua announced, "This is a mystery that I fear not even the great Rockhound can solve."

Rockhound faced his friend. "There's no mystery I can't solve!"

Chihuahua confided, "Wait until you see Madame Mysteriosa. . . she's got to be a fake but nobody knows how she's doing it. I doubt if you'll even be able to figure it out . . . but you've got to be disguised."

Rockhound was about to explode again but his interest had been sparked. "I can solve any mystery. I'll go, but you owe me big. I mean BIG!"

Chihuahua felt the laughter bubbling inside him as he studied Rockhound wearing his disguise of a dress and a wig of long, dark hair. "You look . . ."

"Watch it, buster," Rockhound steamed. "One more word and you can forget this whole crazy deal! How did I ever let you talk me into this?"

Chihuahua avoided looking at Rockhound as they drove to Madame Mysteriosa's house. He explained how Madame Mysteriosa had been getting her customers to give her huge sums of money by allegedly having the spirits answer their questions.

Once inside the ominous looking house, they were seated at a round table. Madame Mysteriosa walked in wearing a midnight-blue robe with silvery celestial symbols. She greeted them with a disarming smile and sat down at the table.

At a signal from Madame Mysteriosa's furry paw, the lights

dimmed to a pale orange, as if from a hidden lantern.

"Observe the glass ball," Chihuahua urged his friend Rockhound, straining to accustom his eyes to the darkness.

Madame Mysteriosa placed her paws on the glass ball on the table. The lights flickered as she chanted, "I call upon the spirits to join us for counsel." She rubbed her paws on the ball as she repeated and repeated her chant.

Rockhound's eyes widened. Something was happening inside the ball. He stared harder and noticed that tiny white figures appeared to be floating under the glass surface of the ball.

Chihuahua poked him, "See that? See that?" His nails were digging into Rockhound's arm.

Madame Mysteriosa seemed to be controlling the figures by moving her paws over the glass ball's surface. Fascinating, Rockhound thought as he watched the tiny figures moving randomly through the air inside the ball.

Suddenly the lights in the room flashed like lightning.

Chihuahua grabbed Rockhound's arm again. "Look! Look up there!"

"Will you cut that out?" Rockhound hissed. He looked up just in time to see two ghost-like figures floating in the air on the far side of the room. They kept moving back and forth toward each other, touching and then pulling away. As they rose toward the ceiling, there was another sudden, blinding flash of light and then the room grew even darker than before.

Rockhound felt his hair stand on end.

"And now," Madame Mysteriosa announced in that strange, hollow voice of hers, "I shall ask the spirits questions, and you shall receive their predictions in the glass ball right before your eyes. Who shall be first?"

Chihuahua asked, "Will my giant tomato win first prize at the police fair?"

"Not your tomatoes again," Rockhound groaned. Chihuahua pinched him to be quiet.

Madame Mysteriosa waved her hand over the glass ball and

9

suddenly the word "yes" appeared on several tiny bits of sparkling paper floating at the top. Chihuahua pinched Rockhound again.

"See that?" he gasped.

"Will you stop pinching me!" Rockhound growled.

"Any other questions?" Madame Mysteriosa asked.

Rockhound smiled sweetly. "I have a question."

"Yes, my dear," Madame Mysteriosa chimed.

Rockhound smiled right into her face and said, "My question is just how will Madame Mysteriosa like spending some time in jail?" Then he ordered the arrest of Madame Mysteriosa and her assistant.

Chihuahua was flabbergasted. What was Rockhound doing?

Mysteriosa gasped indignantly, "What did you say?"

Rockhound ordered, "Arrest that woman. I don't need a crystal ball to predict where you're going to be spending a lot of time."

Reluctantly, Chihuahua ordered the arrest of Madame Mysteriosa and her assistant. Then Chihuahua stormed over to Rockhound. "How could you do that?" he screamed. "How could you place her under arrest before we figured out how she did all those astounding things?"

"What things?" Rockhound asked innocently.

"What things!" Chihuahua yelled. "What things! The ghosts! The spirits! The floating answers! Those things!" he sputtered.

"Oh, those things," Rockhound repeated in an annoyingly calm way.

"I hate it when you do that," Chihuahua ranted.

"Do what?" Rockhound asked, twisting a lock of his wig just to annoy his friend further.

"Do you or don't you know how it was done?" screamed the frustrated Chihuahua.

"Of course I do. Don't you?"
Rockhound loved exasperating his
friend.

Chihuahua stopped screaming.
"You really figured it out?"

"Sure," Rockhound announced
smugly. "It was elementary. Observe
this."

STUDENT PREDICTION PAGE
What do *you* think the outcome will be?
Write your prediction on this page.

_____

_____

_____

_____

_____

_____

_____

_____

_____

_____

AND NOW BACK TO OUR STORY . .

Rockhound picked up the glass ball and rubbed his paw over the surface. Suddenly what looked like ghostly spirits began to rise toward the glass surface. "They're just paper," Rockhound explained as the bits of sparkly paper appeared to dance before Chihuahua's startled face. "Anyone can do it," Rockhound encouraged the captivated Chihuahua to try.

Chihuahua tried rubbing his paw on the glass dome, but the paper inexplicably dropped.

"You have no fur," Rockhound chuckled. "You've no fur."

"So I'm a hairless. You know that," Chihuahua bristled.

"I wasn't insulting you," Rockhound said apologetically. "It just doesn't work without fur. You see, it's all done with static electricity. When you rub fur on the glass, it causes the paper bits to rise."

Chihuahua's mouth dropped open. "Static electricity!" he

14

exclaimed as he slapped his tiny, hairless paw on his forehead. "Of course! Why didn't I think of that?" he wondered out loud. "But how did she make the ghosts move?"

"The ghosts were simply custom designed balloons, which when rubbed by her assistant before-hand, would touch and then repel, and bounce off each other. And the dancing spirits were again bits of paper made to rise when Madame Mysteriosa rubbed them with a furry paw. She used the flash of light to switch glass balls through a concealed door in the table. It was most ingenious, but not supernatural."

"And static electricity made your hair stand on end, right?" Chihuahua asked.

"Yes," Rockhound concurred.

"Ah! Amazing," Chihuahua laughed.

"Not really," Rockhound said with a sly look. "I'd say it was just an electrifying experience."

"It was shocking, even for a hairless pooch like myself!" Chihuahua added, happy that this case was solved.

THE END

ROCKHOUND FILES: ROCKHOUND'S DIRTIEST CASE

It isn't often that Rockhound fails to solve a case . . .

"We need your help," Crystal said, worry filling her puppy face.

"We're here because we have a big problem," Chip, her younger brother sighed.

Rockhound liked these pups, having assisted them in another case. He was surprised to see them in his office again. "What seems to be the trouble?" he asked, wondering what could have upset these pups.

"It's terrible," Chip growled. "They're all dying."

Rockhound frowned. "Who's dying, Chip?"

"The fish," Crystal said in a sullen voice. "The fish at Lazy Bones Lake are all dead or dying."

"And nobody seems to be able to do anything about it," Chip piped up.

"Nobody knows why they're dying," Crystal said, eyeing Chip sternly.

Rockhound was startled. He remembered fishing at the lake as a puppy. It had always been a beautiful site. "I haven't been there for a long time," he said with regret in his voice. "Guess I've been kind of busy."

"Grown-ups are always busy," Chip grumbled.

"Please come with us," Crystal pleaded. "We know you can help."

Rockhound glanced at his clock. He had so many other things to take care of. He shrugged his shoulders and got up from behind his desk full of papers. "Let's go," he said. "Business can wait."

Rockhound drove the pups to the lake. He sighed with relief, "It looks beautiful." He stared at the water framed by what looked like an endless forest of green trees. "It's just as I remembered it. I don't see anything wrong."

Together they followed the shore of the lake for several hundred yards. Rockhound wished that he could spend the rest of the day just wandering in the park. The trees made it feel twenty degrees cooler. The surface of the water looked smooth and clean.

Suddenly Chip's voice shattered the calm. "Look, there's one!" Chip sputtered.

Rockhound saw a dead fish lying in the mud at the side of the lake.

"There aren't many fish left," Crystal sighed. "They're all being killed off."

Rockhound bent down and examined the fish . . . no cuts . . . no wounds at all. "A lot of fish are dying this way?" he inquired.

The puppies nodded. Rockhound studied the water for a long time.

"Could someone be poisoning them?" Crystal asked.

Rockhound bent down and scooped up a pawful of water. "It feels fine," he smiled at the pups. He smelled it. "Nothing I can smell . . . "

"Let's taste it," Chip suggested.

"Don't!" Rockhound replied tersely. "Never taste anything unless you're absolutely sure it's safe."

"Well, what do you think is wrong?" Crystal asked, wondering if Chip was really dumb enough to taste the water.

"We'll soon find out,"

Rockhound said. He collected several samples of water. They looked muddy as he held them to the light. "Pups," he said as he drove them back to his office, "I have a feeling this case isn't going to be an easy case to solve."

"The first thing we need to do is make a filter to get rid of the particles in this water." Rockhound began to scavenge around his office for materials to make a filter. He found a large juice can. He used a hammer and a nail to make tiny holes in the bottom of the can. Then he searched for anything he could use to help screen out the particles of dirt and debris in the muddy water.

Once he packed the can with several layers of filtering materials, Rockhound covered them with a piece of window-screen to catch the largest particles before they reached the filter itself.

Chip and Crystal observed closely as they waited for the muddy water to drip through the filter and into a large glass jar at the bottom. It seemed to take forever, but some water finally passed through to the glass jar.

"I knew you could do it," Chip chirped happily. "That water looks good enough to drink." He grabbed for the water.

"Not so fast," Rockhound cautioned. "This water may look clean, but we still need to test it to see if it is clean. All we've done is taken out the larger particles of dirt. I doubt if dirt was what hurt all those fish." He knew there was more work to do.

Rockhound browsed through his lab boxes until he found a dry cell battery, a light bulb and some wire. He connected the positive side of the dry cell battery to the light bulb and then connected the wire to a metal clip on the glass jar.

"What are you doing?" Chip asked, fascinated by this contraption.

"Are you pretending you're Thomas Edison or someone?" Crystal asked.

"Watch the light bulb," Rockhound said, pleased at having such an attentive audience. He placed the second wire electrode into the water. Suddenly the light bulb lit up.

Rockhound sighed, "I was afraid of that."

"What does it mean?" Chip asked.

Rockhound sadly looked up at the puppy. "It means that this water is polluted . . . but I don't know with what . . . at least not yet."

Chip still looked hopefully at Rockhound. Crystal suddenly looked angry. "What kind of pollution?"

Rockhound did not answer right away. He rummaged around until he found a small container. "This is a box of litmus paper," he said as he opened it. "We can use it to test the water for acid. Litmus paper turns red in an acid solution." Rockhound looked inside to discover the container was empty. "Great," he muttered. "Now I need to think of some other way to find out more about what's killing the fish. Maybe I'll think better after a break. Let's have a snack," he said as he pulled out a couple of cans of juice from the refrigerator. Suddenly he smiled. "Ah! Red cabbage!" he exclaimed.

"Yuck," Chip barked, "I hate red cabbage!" He placed his paws over his mouth as if he were going to throw up.

"Me too," Crystal for once agreed with her brother.

Rockhound laughed. "We're not going to eat it. This cabbage is going to solve our mystery for us."

STUDENT PREDICTION PAGE
What do *you* think the outcome will be?
Write your prediction on this page.

AND NOW BACK TO OUR STORY. . .

"How can yucky red cabbage solve this mystery?" snorted Crystal.

Rockhound asked her to be patient. He began cutting the cabbage into pieces and adding them to a pot of boiling water. He warned the pups never to use a stove without the help of an adult. Boiling water can spill and cause serious burns.

After letting the cabbage cook for a while, he strained off the reddish juice, pouring it into several test tubes and sealing them with corks. "I think we're ready now," he announced. "We'll first do a test with some plain water from the sink, and then with some lemonade, and then milk." Rockhound and the puppies observed as the color of the liquids changed as the cabbage juice was added to them. "Good," he announced, "now we'll try it on our sample from the lake."

Rockhound carefully poured the cabbage juice into the filtered

lake water. The cabbage juice react-
ed exactly as it had done with the
lemonade.

"What does it mean?" Chip asked.

"I'm sad to say my hunch was
right. It means the lake water has
been contaminated with acid,"
Rockhound said with a sigh. "The
fish are dying because the water is
polluted with acid."

"Acid?" Crystal asked, wrinkling her nose with disgust. "Where did the acid come from?"

"Probably from some factory," Rockhound said staring morosely at the discolored liquid.

Chip looked upset. "You can cure it, can't you Rockhound? You can do anything."

Rockhound wished he could make this easier for the pup. He wished he could promise that he would somehow find the polluting factories and make them clean up the lake, but many factories bordered many streams that fed the lake. He knew this problem was so big, many people would have to help to solve it. "I'm afraid I can't cure Lazy Bones Lake," Rockhound said gently. "Not even a great detective can solve the problem of pollution all by himself."

THE END

ROCKHOUND FILES: THE MIDNIGHT RIDE OF ROCKHOUND

It was the Fourth of July, Independence Day. Rockhound always looked forward to this day when many honored the brave animals that had served during America's war for independence. He enjoyed the picnic, the games, the fireworks displays and the reenactment of the midnight ride of Paul Revere's horse.

"Yes," Rockhound hummed, "today is going to be a very special day. Everyone always celebrates the bravery of Paul Revere, but we celebrate the bravery of his horse."

"We've got big trouble," Captain Chihuahua moaned when Rockhound checked in at the station. He handed Rockhound a piece of paper on which were glued words clipped from a newspaper. Rockhound frowned as he read the note:

Hi Rockhead and Captain Ahchoo.
Here's a holiday riddle for you .
One if by land, two if by sea,
How shall your party be ruined by me?
Do watch the sea, and watch the sky,
And forget about celebrating this
Fourth of July!

"Who would dare?" Rockhound growled, crumpling up the note. "Even on a special day like this some low-life crook has to rear his ugly face, let alone his horrible poetry!"

Chihuahua sighed, "I'll have my officers everywhere. It's a shame. They were all looking forward to spending time with their families. Don't crooks have families?"

Rockhound's face was filled with tight-jawed determination. "I tell you now, Captain, no crook is going to ruin this Fourth! I'll help out too!"

Chihuahua sighed, "I knew I could count on you."

Rockhound spent the day checking out all the different areas where festivities were scheduled. He warned the other animals to be aware of any strangers. Wherever he went, the words of the threatening poem kept repeating over and over in his brain.

As the great night approached, Rockhound grew more tense, walking from the parade ground to the picnic area and back again. Nothing seemed unusual . . . everything looked like it was going smoothly. Maybe all the worry was for nothing, he thought.

Suddenly he saw something moving in the field just behind the Canine School. His keen eyes peered into the darkness as he tip-toed on padded paws. Rockhound recognized the two puppies before him as Chip and Crystal. He had helped this brother and sister on another case.

"What are you doing?" Rockhound asked.

"Oh, it's only you," Crystal said with relief.

"Are those fireworks?" Rockhound asked, seeing the packages behind their backs.

"I told you we shouldn't do it," Chip blabbered. "I told you we'd get into trouble."

"Be quiet, Chip," Crystal barked. "Everybody does it."

Rockhound frowned. "Chip is right. You can get into trouble. Fireworks are very dangerous if not handled by professionals. Someone could get badly hurt. I'm sorry, but to protect you, I'm taking your fireworks away." Rockhound became so involved telling the pups about the

dangers of fireworks that he forgot
about the time. " . . . and the rocket
exploded, injuring him," Rockhound
said, "and that's why you shouldn't
handle fireworks." Suddenly he
noticed with alarm that it had grown
dark while he had been talking to

the pups. He glanced at his watch. "Listen pups," he said, "it's getting close to the time for the reenactment of the ride of Paul Revere's horse. I've got to go. There's a threat to the celebration and I've got to protect it."

"Can we help?" Crystal asked.

"Let us go with you!" Chip pleaded, moving closer.

Rockhound knew he could move faster alone, but he didn't want to leave the pups alone, fearing they could get into more trouble. "Okay," he said, "but you have to keep up with me."

"Where are you going?" Crystal asked, running hard.

"I'm not sure," Rockhound called. "Our only clue is a dumb poem."

"Can we hear it?" Chip asked, scampering ahead.

The pups listened carefully as Rockhound recited the poem.

"One if by land, two if by sea," Chip repeated.

"Did you check out the church tower at Old Mill Stream?" Crystal asked.

Rockhound slammed to a stop. "The church!" he said. "Of course! It all starts there. Quick!" he shouted. "I'll run ahead. You meet me at the tower."

Meanwhile, Wily Weasel stared gleefully at the church. "Soon. Soon," he cackled. "My gang is all ready. When they see, I mean, *don't* see the signal lamps, they'll know it's time. Everyone from the town will gather in the park to see the church tower light, and while they wait, . . . and wait, my gang will steal from their houses."

Rockhound reached the base of the tower. Everything looked all right. Everyone in town had arrived and was waiting for the signal lamp to be lit. Once the lamp was shining from the church tower, the people would return to their homes to celebrate with family and friends.

Rockhound raced up the stairs.

The tower guard was slumped on the floor. Rockhound bent down to hear the injured victim say, "Signal . . . signal. Light the lamp."

Rockhound grabbed at the light switch and pulled it down . . . nothing happened. Meanwhile, the townspeople were growing nervous. "Where's the signal?" the mayor hissed to Chihuahua. "Nothing had better go wrong," he warned.

Chihuahua, stuck on the parade stand, gulped.

Chip and Crystal found Rockhound trying to make the switch work. "It's no use," he said. "Something's wrong. I'll never make it."

Weasel laughed. "And now my gang is ready to go."

His pack of crooks waited . . . no light from the tower and off they'd go, knowing that everyone in the town had left their homes unprotected as they waited for the signal lamp in the church tower to light.

Rockhound began to trace the electric wire that led to the lamp. Suddenly he knew what was wrong. Someone had cut and removed a piece of the wire. Rockhound moaned, "There's no time for me to run to town and get another piece to replace what had been taken."

Weasel's gang picked up their bags and tools . . .

Chihuahua felt panic growing as the mayor glared angrily into his face.

"Rockhound, what are you going to do?" Chip asked.

Rockhound stared at the gap in

the wire. If only he could find something that would act as a conductor,
and fill the gap for the few seconds
needed to light the lamp! There had
to be something here that could
work. "We've got to find something
that will conduct electricity." He
began to search the tower…

STUDENT PREDICTION PAGE
What do *you* think the outcome will be?
Write your prediction on this page.

_____

_____

_____

_____

_____

_____

_____

_____

_____

_____

AND NOW BACK TO OUR STORY...

"Quick," Rockhound suddenly commanded, "bring me as many metal forks, spoons or knives as you can find from the church kitchen."

"This is no time for eating," said Crystal.

"Hurry!" Rockhound suddenly ordered as he looked at his watch. "Anything metal . . . especially silver!"

Weasel was staring hard at the tower, greedy foam frothing at his razor teeth. His gang would be off on their crime spree in just a few seconds.

Rockhound picked up a silver fork. "I hope this works," he said, holding the fork with a protective rubber glove. "Never ever fool around with electricity," he warned the pups. "Now, how many signals was it?"

"Two if by sea," Chip continued as he watched Rockhound carefully place the fork in the gap between the wires.

The mayor rose to his feet, his eyes staring at the dark tower. The bulb lit for an instant. Rockhound filled the gap in the wires with the

fork again and the light went on a
second time.

Weasel's gang stopped moving
when they saw the light. Something
had gone wrong . . . the boss hadn't
managed to cut off the power after all.

Weasel flew into a screaming
rage, charging to the tower to find

out what had gone wrong. When he arrived, he ran up the stairs and right into Rockhound.

"I should have guessed it was you," Rockhound said as he grabbed Weasel and cuffed him to a railing.

"But how," Weasel blubbered, "how did you fix the wire?"

Rockhound glared at Weasel. "Not even a criminal genius like you can put out the light of liberty," Rockhound said.

"Not when Rockhound is here," said Chip.

"Not when Chip and Crystal are here," said Rockhound with a proud look at his puppy friend.

THE END

Made in the USA
Middletown, DE
06 January 2017